My Grandma's name is_____

For Mum.
T.T.F.N.

First U.S. edition 1992
First published in Great Britain in 1991 by Walker Books Ltd., London.
Library of Congress Catalog Card Number 91-58747
Library of Congress Cataloging-in-Publication Data
Butterworth, Nick.
My grandma is wonderful / by Nick Butterworth.—1st U.S. ed.
p.   cm.
Summary: Relates the wonderful things Grandma
does, from buying the biggest ice cream cones to always
having what you need in her pocketbook.
ISBN 1-56402-100-9 (pbk.) : $4.95
[1. Grandmother—Fiction.] I. Title.
PZ7.B98225Myd 1992   91-58747
[E]—dc20

10 9 8 7 6 5 4 3 2

Printed in Hong Kong

The illustrations in this book are watercolor.

Candlewick Press
2067 Massachusetts Avenue
Cambridge, Massachusetts 02140

MY GRANDMA IS WONDERFUL

by Nick Butterworth

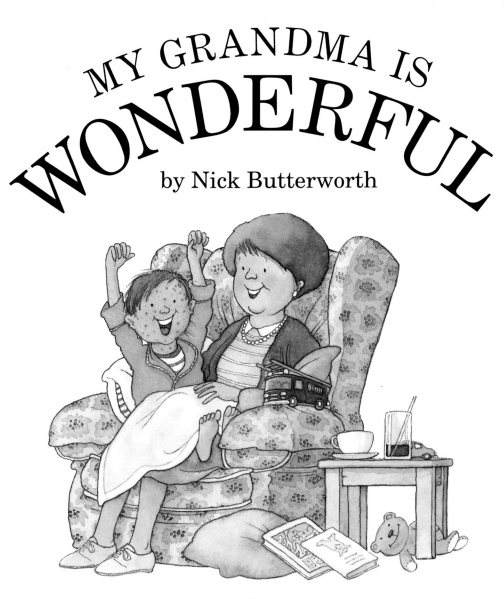

CANDLEWICK PRESS
CAMBRIDGE, MASSACHUSETTS

My grandma is wonderful.

She always buys
the biggest ice-cream cones…

and she never, ever loses
at tic-tac-toe…

and she knows
all about nature...

and she's great at
untying knots...

and she's always
on your side
when things go wrong…

and she makes the most
beautiful clothes...

and when you're sick,
she can make you forget
that you don't feel very good ...

and she can scream
really loudly…

and she has
excellent hearing...

and no matter where you are,
she always has what you need
in her pocketbook.

It's great to have
a grandma like mine.

She's wonderful!